KNIGHT IN TRAINING

SPOTS, STRIPES AND ZIGZAGS

VIVIAN FRENCH
AND DAVID MELLING

For Towerbank Primary, Portobello, with love.
VF

For Iva and Noan Fizir
And in memory of Đuro Sunajko
DM

Dora

Sam J. Butterbiggins
and Dandy the doodlebird

Dennis

Prunella

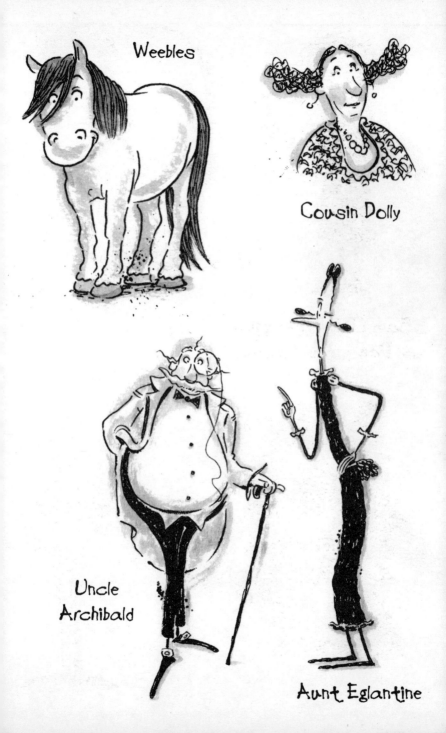

Weebles

Cousin Dolly

Uncle Archibald

Aunt Eglantine

SALTY STEW

Dear Diary,

I've been sent to my room for being rude. Huh! I wasn't rude! At least, I didn't mean to be. All I did was say I didn't want any more stew, and when Aunt Egg asked WHY NOT? I explained it was just a little tiny bit too salty, and she said I was a Very Ungrateful Boy and sent me upstairs! Uncle Archibald winked at me when I passed his chair, so I think he agreed the stew was horrible. It was SO SALTY! I've been drinking LOADS of water, and I'm STILL thirsty.

It's REALLY annoying. Because the cook's gone off to see her poorly grandpa, Aunt Egg made me and Prune help in the kitchen ALL MORNING. We couldn't get to the stable*, so we couldn't read our magic scroll — and that means we still don't know what task we have to do today and it's getting later and later and later ...

(*Maybe we shouldn't have hidden the scroll under Weebles' hay. On the other hand, we can't risk Aunt Egg knowing what we're doing. She doesn't like anything to do with knights; she'd probably confiscate the scroll and use it for lighting the fire or something dreadful like that.)

How am I EVER going to be a Very Noble
Knight, and do Knightly Deeds, if Prune
and I can't do the next task? It's
AFTER LUNCH already, and I'm stuck
here in my room!! Prune's in hers, too.
She wouldn't even try the stew. She
said she'd be sick if she did, and Aunt
Egg went purple and told her she was a
Terrible Disappointment as a daughter.
Prune just skipped off —

"Psssssst!"

Sam jumped, and the doodlebird fell off his shoulder with a squawk as Prune came rushing into the room.

"Quick!" she said. "Pa's dozing in his study, and Ma's snoring in the drawing room, so we can get to the stable without them seeing us. I tiptoed right past Ma and she never even twitched!"

Sam looked anxious. Aunt Egg was Prune's mother, and Prune wasn't afraid of her ... but Sam found his aunt extremely scary, especially

7

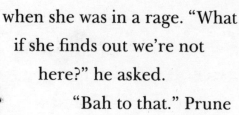

when she was in a rage. "What if she finds out we're not here?" he asked.

"Bah to that." Prune made a face. "She'll never come looking for you, because the stairs make her puff too much. Besides, she'll be going back to the kitchen to concoct some disgusting mess for supper as soon as she wakes up. She was using a cookery book as a blanket."

"Oh dear," Sam said, and Prune giggled.

"I know! She's HOPELESS at cooking!" She fished in her pocket and pulled out an elderly currant bun. "Here. I brought this for you – Pa has a secret stash tucked behind the chest in the hall. I've eaten three. I was STARVING!"

Sam ate the bun gratefully. "Thanks."

Prune looked pleased with herself. "I'm your True Companion, so I have to look after you, Mr Knight-in-training." She headed for the door. "Let's go – and don't make a sound!"

The knight-in-training and his True Companion tiptoed down the tower stairs, the doodlebird flying silently above them. The sound of steady snoring greeted them as they reached the wide hallway and, through the

open drawing-room door, Sam saw his aunt slumped in an armchair clasping a large cookery book to her skinny chest.

"Careful!" Prune warned. Sam nodded, and they crept past, hardly daring to breathe. Once they were on the other side of the doorway they began to run, heading down the long marble corridor towards the kitchen.

"We'll go out the back door!" Prune pointed to the left, and Sam gave her a silent thumbs-up. They rounded the corner at speed and—

CLANG! BANG! CLATTER!

Prune, Sam, Uncle Archibald and a rusty helmet collapsed in a heap.

SCROLL AND SHIELD

Sam was the first to get back on his feet, closely followed by Prune.

"Pa!" she said. "Are you OK?"

Uncle Archibald sat up, clutched the helmet to his chest, and looked guiltily from left to right. "Sh!" he whispered. "Mustn't wake your mother!"

"It's all right, Pa," Prune promised. "She couldn't possibly hear anything. She's snoring too loudly."

Sam was gazing at the helmet with undisguised admiration. "Is that a real knight's helmet, Uncle Archibald?"

His uncle nodded. "Mine, my boy, mine – but it comes from a long time ago, what what what. Silly to keep it. Sentimental, and your aunt doesn't approve. Not at all."

"But what were you doing with it?" Prune wanted to know.

Her father looked even more guilty. "Wear it from time to time. Memories, you know. Memories."

"So have you got a whole suit of armour?" Sam asked, his eyes shining. "And a lance? And a shield?"

"Goodness me, no." Uncle Archibald was shocked by the suggestion. "Gave all that to the cousins. Couldn't keep it here." He gave the helmet a wistful stroke. "Should get rid of this as well. Send it to Puddlewink Castle. LOADS of this stuff at Puddlewink. Helmets, swords, shields, lances. Loads and loads of it."

Sam looked hopeful. A castle full of knightly armour sounded like his very best dream come true. "Would you like us to take it there for you, Uncle Archibald?"

Uncle Archibald sighed heavily. "Kind of you, dear boy, but it wouldn't do. Can't have you upsetting your aunt."

"Why would it upset Aunt Egg?" Sam was mystified.

Prune stuck an elbow in his side. "Silly – you know what Ma's like about knights and armour and Noble Deeds! She hates all that kind of thing. She says we ought to look to the future.

And she really really REALLY hates Cousin
Dolly, because Dolly was rescued from being
eaten by a dragon by a Very Noble Knight,
and Dolly's still talking about it, even though
it was about a hundred years ago. And the
dragon's probably talking about it too, because
he'd have got TERRIBLE indigestion if he'd
eaten her. She's all bones and whiskers."

There was such a
loud rumble from Uncle
Archibald that Sam looked
at him in alarm before
realising his uncle was
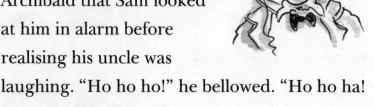
laughing. "Ho ho ho!" he bellowed. "Ho ho ha!
Ho ho hah ha—"

"ARCHIE? Archibald – where are you? And
why are you laughing like that?"

There was no doubt that the voice echoing
down the corridor belonged to Aunt Eglantine.

Uncle Archibald's laugh cut off mid
HAH, and Sam gasped.

Prune dived forward, grabbed the helmet
with one hand, and Sam's arm with the other.
"RUN!" she hissed.

"AWK!" agreed the doodlebird. "AWK!"

Sam needed no further encouragement. He
and Prune shot away from the approaching
footsteps, and dashed through the back door
into the sunshine.

"PHEW!" Sam stopped to catch his breath. "That was close!"

"Poor old Pa." Prune shook her head. "Still, at least Ma won't catch him cuddling a helmet."

Sam grinned. "No. And we can hide it in the stable. Come on! I can't wait to see what the scroll has to say!"

Keeping a careful eye out for a rampaging Aunt Egg, Sam and Prune made their way round the back of the castle to the stable. There they found Dora, Sam's snow-white steed, fast asleep. Prune's pony, Weebles, was looking hopefully out of his stall.

"Good boy," Prune said as she gave him an approving pat. "We'll be off and away any minute now. Can you find the scroll, Sam?"

Sam was hunting under the hay in Weebles' manger. "Here it is," he said as he pulled out

the ancient parchment.
Prune leant against
Weebles' solid body,
and Sam carefully
unrolled their
most precious
possession.

The doodlebird perched on a beam, and
peered down with interest.

"Greetings to all who wish
to be Truly Noble Knights,"
Sam read out loud. "Herewith
we offer you the tasks that should be accomplished,
in order as hereby listed, that ye may succeed ..."

Prune clicked her tongue impatiently. "Get
to today's task," she told him. "I know that bit
off by heart."

"The letters haven't come through yet," Sam said. "It's beginning to feel warm, though. In fact it's— OUCH!" He dropped the scroll, and rubbed his fingers. "Watch out! Don't pick it up yet – it's really hot!"

Prune and Sam stared down at the parchment lying on the straw by their feet. A wisp of smoke floated up, and the letters glowed bright gold.

"I can read it from here," Prune said. "Go forth and earn thy knightly shield. Choose well; thy shield is thine, and thine alone, but many are the number all about it. Look for the beginnings that have no end, and remember thy number is one hundred and eleven. Put these together, add thy letter (which is last of all) and thou hast found thy shield."

There was a silence while both Prune and Sam studied the words. Already the gleam of gold was fading, and the letters were growing fainter and fainter.

"Um," Sam said, and he scratched his head. "What does it mean? I can't do riddles."

"It looks as if it's cooled down now." Prune picked the scroll off the ground and rolled it up again. "I'm no good at riddles either, but there's one pretty obvious clue."

"Really?" Sam looked at her hopefully, and Prune nodded.

"You remember it said, 'Many are the number all about it'? That's easy peasy!"

"I didn't understand that bit either." Sam watched as Prune put the scroll back in its hiding place. "Unless it meant there were loads of other shields."

Prune snorted. "Of course it did! And we know exactly where there are loads of shields, don't we – so all we have to do is go and find yours!"

WINKING TOADS

Sam's brain was whirring. *Did* he know where there were loads of shields? He couldn't think of anywhere, and Prune wasn't giving anything away. She was leading Weebles out of his stall, deliberately ignoring Sam. He scratched his head again, and looked up at the doodlebird. "Do *you* know, Dandy?" he whispered.

The doodlebird leant down.

"AWK."

"YES!" Sam gave Dandy a grateful smile, and called out, "Puddlewink Castle!"

"Wooooeee!"

29

Prune gave an exaggerated sigh. "So your brain DOES work. I was beginning to wonder. Puddlewink is Cousin Dolly's castle, and I've always wanted to go there … I went with Pa when I was little, and it was brilliant! But Ma throws a purple fit every time I ask about going, and I didn't want to go on my own. Hurry up and get Dora ready!"

Sam did as he was told. As he saddled and bridled the big white horse he was thinking about the scroll, trying to remember what it had said.

"I do wish the tasks were easier to understand," he said as he and Dora joined

Prune and Weebles in the stable yard. "A 'beginning that has no end'. It doesn't make any sense!"

"Maybe that's the point of it," Prune suggested. "I mean, maybe you've got to be able to untangle riddles as part of your training to be a knight."

"You're probably right," Sam agreed. He looked round as they rode out of the yard, half expecting to see an angry Aunt Egg rushing out of the castle. "Is it far to Puddlewink? Will we be back before your mother notices we've gone?"

Prune shook her head at him. "Honestly, Sam! You are SUCH a worry wart! No, it's not that far. Well – not if we get a move on. Ma'll be chopping up cabbages and onions and things for hours, and as long as we're back in time for supper she'll never know we haven't been inside all afternoon."

"OK," Sam said, but he heaved a huge sigh of relief as they left the castle grounds behind them. He suspected Prune felt the same as she began to hum, and Weebles and Dora broke into a cheerful trot. Even the doodlebird burst into song.

"AWK!" he sang. "AWK AWK AWK AWK!"

Prune was right. Puddlewink Castle wasn't very far away. A little more than an hour's fast riding brought them to an overgrown, treelined driveway, with two tall pillars on either side of a rusty gate that was hanging off its hinges. Each pillar was topped with an extremely ugly toad, balancing

on one leg, and both toads were winking at Sam with a leer that reminded him of the unfortunate portrait of his parents.

Prune saw him staring at the toads. "Puddle wink," she explained. Toads were called puddles in the old days ... at least, that's what Pa told me."

"Ummm," Sam said. "They don't look very friendly."

Prune laughed. "They're not meant to. Great Great Great Grandfather Backstepper put them up, and he hated

everyone. But it's OK now. Cousin Dolly's mad, but she loves visitors. And she'll be thrilled to pieces that we've brought something for her collection." She patted Uncle Archibald's rusty helmet.

Sam took a deep breath. He and Prune

were doing a Good Deed. In fact, two Good Deeds. They had saved Uncle Archibald from Aunt Egg, and now they were going to make an old lady happy. But the scroll had said he needed to earn his shield. Were good deeds enough? He wasn't sure.

"Watch out for the bats," Prune warned him as they made their way carefully over the ruts and bumps. "They've been trained to—"

"OUCH!" Sam jumped as a small bat whizzed out of nowhere and slapped him in the face with its little leathery wing. "That hurt!" He brushed the bat away, only to be

dive bombed by another, and another. He was
saved by the doodlebird, who came zooming
after them squawking fiercely.

"Thanks, Dandy," Sam said gratefully.
He looked to see if Prune was all right, and
saw she was waving her arms in the air and
muttering something.

"What are you doing?" he asked.

"SH!" Prune shushed him. "I'm trying to
remember the words. Pa said something that
made the bats realise he was— OUCH!"

It was Prune's turn to be slapped. "Go
AWAY, you horrible things!" she shouted.
"I'm Princess Prunella, and this is Sam J.
Butterbiggins, and the Honourable Dollianna
Backstepper is our COUSIN!"

The bats twittered questioningly to each
other, then flew round Prune's head in a circle.

Sam, watching, had a flash of inspiration. "Show them the helmet!"

Prune did as she was told, and the bats circled once more, whistled their approval, then flittered away.

"Good thinking, Sam," Prune told him. "Weren't they horrid?"

"Yes," Sam agreed, but he wasn't listening to his cousin. They had ridden round a sharp bend in the driveway, and his eyes were fixed on the castle that was now in front of him. Four towers soared into the air, with tattered flags flying from the battlements and a rusted weather vane at the top of each tower. The windows were cracked and covered in cobwebs,

and ivy curled up the walls and right up to the roof. "Is that where we're going?" he asked.

"It's not half as bad as it looks." Prune

waved a hand at the castle. "Cousin Dolly lives in the bottom, and it's quite comfortable. Only the uncles live in the top bit with the bats."

"The uncles?" Sam asked. "You never said anything about uncles."

"They're really great great uncles," Prune explained. "They're triplets, and they're about a hundred and fifty years old. Uncle Rodney, Uncle Lionel and Uncle Adolphus."

"Oh." Sam's attention had wandered again. The drive had led them to a drawbridge, and he was inspecting it doubtfully. "Is that safe, do you think? There are an awful lot of planks missing."

"There are, aren't there," Prune agreed. "And the water looks horribly murky. Maybe we should leave Weebles and Dora here, and we can go over on foot. There's masses of grass – they'll be fine."

The doodlebird flew down to Sam's shoulder. "AWK?"

Sam nodded as he slid off Dora's wide back. "Dandy says he'll stay here and keep an eye on them," he told Prune. "We can whistle if we need him." He reached up to pat Dora's neck fondly. "Good girl. Stay here and wait for me."

The huge white horse nodded, and plodded away to where the grass was thick and green. The doodlebird settled himself

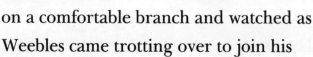

on a comfortable branch and watched as Weebles came trotting over to join his companion, and Sam and Prune made their way towards the drawbridge.

On the other side was the front entrance to Puddlewink Castle – a heavy iron portcullis protecting a massively studded wooden door. But Sam could see a gap below the portcullis, and the door was propped open with a stone.

"Let's see …" Sam put a cautious foot on the first plank.

"Oh NO!"

The ancient wood crumbled into dust, and the dirty green water in the moat below swirled and surged. As Sam and Prune stared in horror a pair of viciously sharp-toothed jaws snapped at the empty air, and a voice croaked, "HUNGRY! HUNGRY!"

"I don't remember THAT," Prune said. "What do you think it is?"

Sam shook his head. "No idea. But I don't

want to be its dinner ..."

"Me neither," Prune said. "How on earth are we going to get to the castle?"

HIGGLEDY
PIGGLEDY

"Coooeeee!" It was a very different voice, and it was coming from a small open window above the front door. "Could that possibly be my darling Prunella? All grown up? Dearest one – what a joy to see you! But don't try and cross that silly old bridge. Dennis hasn't had his tea yet, and he's just a little bit tetchy."

"Cousin Dolly!" Prune waved the helmet in the air. "Hello! We've brought you a helmet! It used to belong to Pa, but he doesn't need it any more. How do we get to you if we can't cross over the moat?"

"Go round the back!" Cousin Dolly pointed away from the moat. "So much easier, and Dennis can't reach. SUCH a naughty boy! He gobbled up the postbag only last week. Who's your little friend, darling one?"

Prune pushed Sam forward. "Sam J. Butterbiggins, knight-in-training. I'm his True Companion, Cousin Dolly, and we're looking for a shield."

"How absolutely wonderful." Cousin Dolly sounded genuinely enthusiastic. "DO hurry, darlings, and we'll see what we can find; I've got plenty for you to choose from. You'll have tea first, of course. I'll run and put the kettle on …" And the window shut.

"Come on, Sam," Prune said. "Let's find the back way …" She paused, and peered at his face. "What's the matter?"

Sam rubbed his head. "I was just wondering … do you think we ought to have told her we were looking for a shield?"

"Of course we should." Prune frowned. "We can't just walk in and help ourselves, can we? It wouldn't be polite!"

"But I don't think your cousin ought to just give us a shield. I'm sure we have to earn it, somehow." Sam was having difficulty explaining his feelings. "That's what the scroll said. And it has to be the right one, too. All that stuff about one hundred and eleven, and beginnings that have no end …"

"Don't be such an old fuss-pot," Prune

said cheerfully, and she led the way along the
path that circled the moat and the castle. Sam
heaved a sigh, and followed her. Much to his
alarm Dennis swam beside him, every so often
opening his enormous jaws and growling,

"HUNGRY!" to remind Sam and the world that he hadn't had his tea. It was with relief that Sam saw a small but solidly built bridge arching high over the moat and leading directly to the back door of the castle. He and Prune hurried across as Dennis growled his disapproval from below.

"Coooeee! Cousin Dolly! We're here!" Prune called as they stepped inside a large and chaotic kitchen. Books, papers, pots, pans and plates were piled higgledy piggledy against the walls, and an enormous Welsh dresser was groaning under the weight of the miscellaneous items crammed on to every shelf. A half knitted scarf was wrapped round a baby's potty, a glass tumbler filled with false teeth grinned amongst half eaten jars of marmalade, several bottles of dubious looking dandelion wine were tucked into an upturned top hat, and boxes and boxes of herbs and spices were balanced precariously in between hundreds of rusty tin cans and cracked china teapots. A couple of canaries trilled happy songs from a roof beam hung with faded ribbons and twists of string, while beneath them a kettle puffed clouds of steam from an iron range that looked as if it might well be older than the castle itself.

Cousin Dolly had been busy; Sam's stomach rumbled as he saw the huge wooden table covered with plates of fruit cake, sponge cake, coffee cake and chocolate cake, bowls of red, green and orange jelly, and trays and trays of sandwiches, iced buns and biscuits.

There was a rattle of plates, and Dolly popped out of a cupboard. "There you are at last, my darlings! I was just beginning to

wonder if that naughty Dennis had snapped
you up. DO remind me to feed him before
you go home. When he gets really REALLY
hungry he crawls out of the moat, and it's such
a problem getting him to go back because his
poor little paws dry out and then he has to
be carried."

The thought of Dennis crawling out of
the moat almost made Sam lose his appetite.

"I'll remind you," he said. "I PROMISE."

"Thank you, darling." Cousin Dolly gave him an approving smile. "What a poppet you are!

"And Prune ... what a simply splendid addition to my collection." She took Uncle Archibald's rusty helmet and hung it on the wall.

"Wow!" Prune was looking at the spread on the table. "That looks wonderful."

Her cousin pulled out two chairs. "Sit yourselves down, and I'll make the tea. When you've finished you can take some cake up to the uncles, and have a look at the shields along the way. If you can't find what you're looking for you must ask Uncle Rodney – he knows EVERYTHING about our shields. Make sure you ask him BEFORE he has his cake, though.

Eating makes him go to sleep almost at once."

Sam and Prune nodded, and settled themselves down to the enormous tea.

"Were you expecting a lot of people to come today?" Sam asked as he helped himself to a large slice of chocolate cake. "There's enough here for a party!"

Cousin Dolly put her head on one side. "What I say is, you never know who might call in, so always be ready!"

Sam couldn't answer. He was having trouble with his first bite. The cake was rock solid,

and he suspected that it was not just old, but ancient. Extremely ancient.

Prune was grappling with an iced bun. "Cousin Dolly," she said, "when did you make this?"

Cousin Dolly gave a merry laugh. "Who knows, darling? Last year, was it? Or maybe it's one my grandmother made. I really can't remember. I keep them all, you see. Can't bear to throw anything useful away. Try that one over there – the coffee one. That's VERY new."

Both Prune and Sam did as she suggested, and found she was right. It was actually possible to eat the coffee cake, although it was still far from fresh.

"Delicious," Sam lied as he washed the last of the stale crumbs down with a swig of tea. "But it's VERY filling. I don't think I can eat anything else, thank you."

"Nor me," Prune agreed. "Cousin Dolly, is it OK if we go and look at the shields now?"

Cousin Dolly was looking disappointed. "But darlings! You haven't even touched the jellies! Won't you try just a spoonful of wibble wobble? Dennis adores jelly – he's got a VERY sweet tooth – but I hardly ever let him have any. Visitors first, you see."

Sam didn't want to seem rude. "Perhaps we could have some later," he suggested. "They do look … erm … very colourful."

Prune, who seldom bothered with politeness, was already on her feet. "Come on, Sam. We'll be back soon, Cousin Dolly."

"Don't forget the uncles, darling!" Cousin Dolly picked up a large knife

and, with some difficulty, cut three slices of
chocolate cake. These she placed on a solid
silver tray together with three dusty jam tarts,
three aged sausages and three sad-looking
custard slices, before handing the tray to Sam.
"Darling boy – do remind them to put their
teeth in before they eat. And hurry back for
your lovely tea."

"Of course," Sam said, and he followed
Prune out of the kitchen and through a
broken-down arch that led to the great hall.

UNCLE MUSIC

"WOW!" Sam turned round and round, staring. The walls were covered from floor to ceiling in shields, swords, helmets and other assorted bits of armour. Some were so rusted that it was a miracle they hadn't crumbled away, but others still gleamed and shone.

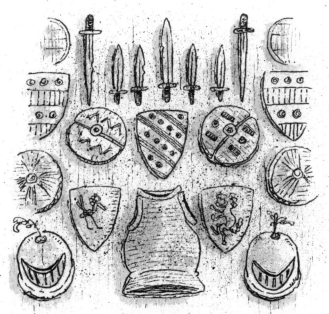

"Pa's old helmet'll look great here." Prune pointed at the walls. "Now, can you see any shields that look as if they have numbers on?"

Sam shook his head. "There are LOADS! It'll take for ever to look at them all!"

"Rubbish," Prune said. "We just need a plan. You take the left hand side and I'll take the right ... What's the matter? You've got your dead fish face on. Have you got a better idea?"

"Couldn't we take your uncles their tea first?" Sam asked. His arms were beginning to ache under the weight of the silver tray, and it was difficult to combine balancing the cakes with studying the walls. "Then we can look properly on the way down."

He had half expected Prune to tell him off for being feeble, but after a moment's consideration she nodded. "OK. And we can ask them what they think we should be looking

for. Pa says they were all knights about a
hundred years ago."

"Really?" Sam felt better at once. Even if the
uncles were hugely old they might well have
interesting knightly stories to tell. He gripped
the silver tray more firmly and set off for the
stairs at the far end of the hall.

Prune didn't immediately
follow him. She was standing
with her hands behind her back,
staring upwards. Sam, reaching
the first flight of stairs, turned
to see what she was doing.

"Are you coming?" he
asked.

"I think," Prune said
slowly, "I might be even
cleverer than I thought I
was. I think I might actually be a genius."

Sam snorted. "Is that right?"

Prune took no notice of his snort. "Look at that row of shields ... the ones near the top. What have they all got on them?"

With a sigh, Sam took a couple of steps back into the hall and peered upwards. "Circles," he said.

"Exactly!" Prune nodded. "And how do you draw a circle?"

"With a pencil?" Sam guessed.

His cousin frowned at him. "No, stupid. Think about it! What do you actually DO? You begin by drawing a curvy line, and then you join it up to make a circle – so there isn't really an end at all ... a circle just goes round and round and ROUND!"

It took Sam a long moment to understand what she was saying, but gradually an enormous grin spread over his face. "So my shield has circles on it?"

"Circles … or spots," Prune agreed.

"Wowee! You ARE a genius!" If Sam hadn't been carrying a heavy tray he'd have clapped Prune on the back. As it was, he could only smile, but that was enough. Prune, delighted with her own brilliance, smiled back.

"It'll make it loads and LOADS easier," she said. "We can ignore all the ones with weird birds and animals, and concentrate on the spotty ones and the ones with circles. Aren't you lucky you've got such a clever True Companion?" She paused for more congratulations, but none came. "Sam? SAM! Are you listening?"

It was Sam's turn to stare at the shields.
Circles and spots were very popular. Very
popular indeed. It was true that a few had
only birds, or animals, but the majority had a
spot or a circle somewhere in their design. In
fact, Sam was beginning to wonder if Prune's
idea was as helpful as she
was making out. "There
are spots with almost
everything," he thought.
"It's a shame it wasn't
stripes. There aren't
nearly as many of
those." He sighed,
and went back up
the steps wondering if
he would ever find his very own shield. "I just
hope these uncles can help. Otherwise we'll be
here for days and days and DAYS …"

Prune wasn't moving. She was still looking at the display of armour and gloating over her discovery.

"Come on," Sam called over his shoulder. "My arms are about to fall off!"

Prune made a face. "Jealous," she muttered as she stomped after him. "He's wishing he was as clever as me."

The stairs were steep and winding, and the staircase grew gradually narrower and narrower. There were very few windows, and it became increasingly difficult to see; spiders' webs trailed down and tickled Sam's nose, and made him sneeze. Every so often a sudden squeak followed by scuttling noises made him wonder if he was disturbing families of rats. "A knight-in-training is NOT afraid of rats,"

he told himself, and he clutched the tray more
firmly and staggered on.

Prune, a few steps
behind him, was still
thinking about her
extreme cleverness. "What
would Sam do without me?
I'm the best True Companion there ever—

AAAAAAAAAGH!"

A large rat was heading down
the stairs towards her. Prune's
scream frightened it so much
that it swung round to rush back
to where it had come from, and got tangled in
Sam's feet. Sam, the tray and everything on it
crashed to the ground, and cakes of various
descriptions bounced down the steps.

"Oh NO!" Sam was on his hands and knees.
Prune came up the stairs towards him, picking

up food as she went and keeping a wary eye
out for the rat.

"The jam tarts and sausages are OK,"
she reported. "I can only find two slices of
chocolate cake, though, and I can't see the
custard slices anywhere."

"They're here," Sam said. "I trod on one,
and it was so hard it didn't even squish.
But why did you scream like that? What
happened?"

Prune looked vague while she tried to think of a reason. She didn't want to confess that she was frightened of rats, and she was most unwilling to admit it was her fault Sam had dropped the tray. "Oh ... erm ... I was just practising. In case you ever needed me to scream. To ... to frighten ghosts, or something."

Sam looked surprised. "Really? I thought you might have seen a rat ... they're everywhere." He shuddered. "I hate them."

For a moment Prune felt guilty, but she managed to ignore her better self quite easily. "It's a good thing you've got me to look after you, then, isn't it? Come on. I can see a light up above us, and I can hear music – that'll be the uncles!"

UBBLE UBBLE

To call the noise coming from the top floor of
the castle music was extremely flattering. Sam's
ears buzzed as he listened. There was definitely
a trumpet, and as he came up the stone steps
he recognised the ping ping ping! of a triangle
… but there was a third sound that he hadn't
ever heard before.

"What's making that
ooooomph oooooomph noise?"
he asked Prune. "It's making
my ears ache!"

Anyone who had ever heard
Prune play the bagpipes hoped very much
never to hear her play again. Now she looked
up at Sam with a smile. "That's Uncle Lionel's

Gufflehorn! Isn't it lovely?"

Sam blinked, but before he had time to
argue Prune hopped in front of him and
heaved open a small wooden door at the top of
the stairs. Immediately the noise grew twice as
loud; if Sam hadn't been carrying a large tray

he would have clapped his hands to his ears. Fortunately his and Prune's arrival distracted the musicians, and a sudden silence fell.

"Hello, great uncles!" Prune said. "It's me! Prunella! And this is Sam J. Butterbiggins, knight-in-training. I'm his True Companion, and I look after him and make sure he isn't frightened by rats and stuff like that. Cousin Dolly sent us up with some tea for you, and we want to ask you about shields."

Sam balanced the tray on top of a pile of books, and stretched his aching arms. "Good afternoon," he said politely.

The tallest uncle put down his triangle. "Wheels? Wheels?" His voice was thin and quavery. "Wheelie wheelie wheelie WOO!" He emphasised the final WOO! with a PING! on his triangle, and Sam's heart sank. He looked hopefully at the next uncle, but the trumpet player was already inspecting the plates of sausages and cakes. He was either ignoring Prune or, as Sam suspected, was even deafer than his brother.

Uncle Lionel, who was small and round as a ball, was disentangling himself from the serpentine coils of the Gufflehorn. When he finally emerged he blew his nose loudly before grinning a toothless grin at Sam and Prune. "Deaf as posts, those two. No good talking to them. Might as well talk to the trumpet." He stopped to wheeze heavily. "Oooeeee! Gufflehorn takes a chap's breath away. What did you want? Shields?"

"Yes please." Sam nodded. "Erm ... we're looking for one shield in particular, but we don't know what it looks like."

"It's got spots or circles on it," Prune said. "I worked that out. A 'beginning that has no end'. That's a circle, you see. Or a spot. You draw a line and—"

"SPOTS?" Uncle Lionel shouted, and Sam and Prune jumped. "Not spots, child! T'chah! Never call 'em spots! Or circles. *Circlets*, that's the word. Circlets. And you Archie's daughter, and him a Noble Knight! T'chah!"

The tallest uncle waved his triangle. "Spotty spotty dotty dotty," he sang. "Ziggy zigzag one one one, growly wowly fun fun fun—"

"Silence, Rodney!" Great Uncle Lionel ordered, then shook his head. "Poor old Rodders. Overexcited. Used to know every shield in the country. And beyond! Brain's a bird's nest these days. No sense at all."

"There aren't any birds on Sam's shield," Prune said. "There was a number, though. And a letter. What was it, Sam? 'The last of all', whatever that means."

Great Uncle Lionel looked disapproving. "No such thing as numbers in heraldry. Nor letters. Not done. Not at all!"

"Oh." Prune looked gloomily at Sam. "Did you hear that? What shall we do now? Sam? SAM?"

Her cousin was standing staring at Great Uncle Rodney, his mouth wide open. When Prune elbowed him sharply, he gulped. "Please," he said to Rodney, "please could you sing that again?"

"Ubble ubble," Great Uncle Rodney said helpfully. "Ubble ubble?"

"SING, RODDERS!"

Playing the Gufflehorn had evidently
strengthened Uncle Lionel's lungs,
and Rodney brightened.

"Spotty spotty dotty dotty. Ziggy
zigzag one one one, growly wowly fun fun
fun."

"That's it!" Sam breathed. "One and one
and one is how you write hundred and eleven,
and a zigzag is how you write Z – and Z is the
last letter in the alphabet! THAT'S what's on
my shield! A circle, a letter Z, and one one
one!"

Prune snorted. "Don't talk rubbish! Great
Uncle Lionel just said you don't get numbers
on shields."

"But you do get stripes!" Sam was pink with
excitement. "I saw them on the shields in the
hall! Some had one stripe, some two ... and

a few had three!" He turned to Great Uncle
Lionel. "That's what Great Uncle Rodney
meant, wasn't it? A shield with a – what was it
you said? Oh yes. A circlet, a zigzag and three
stripes!"

Lionel stroked his bristly chin. "Didn't catch

the words first time round. But you're right.
Old birdbrain must have seen it. Wouldn't sing
a song about it if he hadn't."

Sam was quivering with excitement. "So is it
here? In this room?"

Great Uncle Lionel shrugged. "Must be. We
never go anywhere else. Now, what's this tea

you've brought us? Chocolate cake, eh? Looks
a bit dusty. Drop it on the way, did you?"

"I'm very sorry," Sam apologised, but Lionel
just laughed. "Old as the hills, Dolly's cakes.
No matter. Still tasty. Come on, chaps! Dig in!"
And he pulled a set of gleaming white false
teeth out of his pocket, slapped them into his
mouth, and began eating. His brothers joined
him, their visitors of no further interest.

Sam and Prune looked at each other.

"What do we do now?" Sam whispered.

"Find the shield, of course, silly!" Prune whispered back, and the two of them began searching the room. There were shields hanging on the walls, but more were on the floor being used as holders for dead pot plants, or to prop up three-legged tables, or as containers for old socks or broken spectacles. The knight-in-training and his True Companion inspected every shield they found … but after a solid hour of looking it was clear that it was no good. The spotty zigzag three-striped shield wasn't there.

"Someone must have moved it." Sam drooped.

"There's only one person who could have taken it out of here, and that's Cousin Dolly," Prune said. "It must be downstairs. Come on! Let's go and ask her where she put it!"

DENNIS IS
HUNGRY

Sam was hardly able to breathe for excitement
as he and Prune hurried down the winding
stone steps. They ran through the great hall,
jumped through the broken arch and arrived,
panting, in the kitchen – to find Cousin Dolly
standing on the kitchen table. The cakes,
sandwiches, jellies and biscuits were gone;
only empty plates remained, together with the
sugar bowl and the salt
and pepper pots.

"What on earth—"
Prune began, but she was
interrupted.

"HUNGRY! HUNGRY!

HUNGRY!"

Dennis was framed in the back door, his mouth wide open. Crumbs of cake on the floor and smears of chocolate around his scaly cheeks explained the empty plates, but it was all too obvious that he was wanting more. When he saw Sam and Prune his little black eyes lit up, and he oozed further into the kitchen. "HUNGRY!"

"I'd suggest the table, darlings," Cousin Dolly said, but Prune and Sam were already up beside her. One look at Dennis's teeth had been enough to send them scrambling for safety.

"I don't know what's got into him," Cousin Dolly sighed. "He's normally such a sweetheart. He must have been extra specially hungry ... look! He's eaten everything! And now he wants more, and there isn't anything left. But it's all my fault. I've been meaning and meaning to feed him, and I even found him a lovely new bowl ... but I never got round to it. And now look at him!"

Sam was looking. In fact, he was staring. Dennis was the nearest thing to a dragon he had ever seen, and he was wondering whether he would ever be brave enough to tackle a real life-sized dragon head on. "But that's what real true knights do," he told himself. "And I'm going to be a Very Noble Knight. Well, just as soon as I can finish all my tasks. But I'm here now … and getting Dennis to go back to his moat would be a Very Good Deed. And I need to do Very Good Deeds. But how?"

Prune was also staring at Dennis, who was now licking up the crumbs with a long green tongue. "Can he climb things?" she asked.

Cousin Dolly trilled with laughter. "Climb? Oh, NO, darling. Whatever made you think that? You're absolutely safe up here."

"He did climb out of the moat," Prune pointed out. Dennis looked up at her, and she wriggled further away from the edge of the table. As she did so she knocked over the salt pot. Sam put out a hand to pick it up … and froze. "SALT!" he said.

"That's right, darling," Cousin Dolly agreed. "Sugar, salt and pepper. I always put them out for my lovely visitors. Of course, my cooking never needs anything extra, but I think it's polite to offer it."

"Salt," Sam said again, and a vision of Aunt Egg's salt-laden stew floated into his mind. He had been thirsty ever since eating it; he was thirsty now. And it was giving him an idea … a GOOD idea … at least, he hoped it was.

He picked up the sugar bowl, and leant over the edge of the table. "Here! Dennis! Here boy! Something nice!"

As Dennis came closer, Sam poured sugar on to the floor. Dennis tried it cautiously, then began enthusiastically licking it up.

"Darling!" Cousin Dolly protested. "That's VERY bad for his toothies! Do please stop doing that!"

Sam didn't answer. He was now adding salt to the sugar; Dennis didn't notice. It wasn't until he had eaten the entire contents of both the sugar bowl and the salt pot that he sat back, looking puzzled. He licked his lips, then licked them again.

"Thirsty," he said plaintively. "THIRSTY!"

Sam pointed at the back door. "Lots of water in the moat, Dennis. Lovely water!"

"THIRSTY!"

Dennis shook his heavy head.

"THIRSTY!" And with a heave of his enormous body he turned himself round and lumbered out of the door.

A moment later there was a mighty SPLASH! followed by loud slurping and gulping noises.

Two moments later a voice said, "HAPPY."

Three moments later there was the sound of damp snoring.

Cousin Dolly looked at Sam. "That was very clever of you, darling – but generally speaking you really shouldn't give a pet sugar. Or salt. All the same, you've done a good deed, and I'm very grateful. Now – what on earth am I going to give you for your tea? Dennis has eaten everything on the table. I'll just run and look in the cupboard …"

As Cousin Dolly climbed off the table and pattered away, Prune grinned at Sam. "Don't tell me. Let me guess! Ma's stew made you think of doing that!"

Sam blushed. "Yes. Sorry."

Prune laughed. "Must be the first time her cooking's had a good result." She stretched, and jumped down on to the floor. "Why are you looking like a dead fish? That's the second time today."

"Sorry." Sam shrugged. "I was thinking about my shield. I've been looking, and I'm sure it isn't here."

"Rubbish," Prune said. "You haven't been looking at all. You've just been staring round. I bet it's underneath a pile of plates or something. Look – here's Cousin Dolly coming back! Ask her!"

Cousin Dolly was staggering under the

weight of an enormous fruit cake. "I was saving this for Christmas," she said, "but we'll have it now. Prune, my darling … pop the kettle back on." Sam crossed his fingers behind his back, and leant forward.

"Cousin Dolly," he said, "did you by any chance bring a shield down from the great uncles' attic? It has spots and stripes and zigzags on it. I think it might be the one I'm looking for."

"A shield, darling?" Cousin Dolly crashed the cake on to the table. "I can't say I remember picking one up."

"Are you quite sure?" Prune asked. "It's really important!"

Cousin Dolly stared into space. "A shield … spots, stripes and zigzags. It does ring the very faintest bell, darling, but I can't for the life of me think why."

Prune sighed, and went to put the kettle on. "Think VERY HARD, Cousin Dolly!"

"Please," Sam begged. "PLEASE!"

Cousin Dolly sat down, and closed her eyes. "I'm thinking, darlings," she explained. "Now … what have I been doing recently? Let me see …"

There was a long silence, and Prune and Sam waited anxiously.

"What was I doing when I was last in the attic?" Cousin Dolly rubbed her nose. "I took the uncles some wibbly wobbly jelly, I do remember that. And I meant to take Dennis

some too, because he was swimming round his
moat going 'Growly wowly growly wowly', and
it was so funny! I told the great uncles – had
to shout, of course – and HOW they laughed!
But –" Cousin Dolly looked guilty – "I never
remembered to take poor Dennis any. And I'd
found him a special dish, as well, but I never
gave it to him—"

"That's it!" Sam was purple in the face
with excitement. "Where's the dish? PLEASE,
Cousin Dolly … where is it? Because that's
what Uncle Rodney sang … 'Growly wowly fun

fun fun', so he MUST have been thinking of
Dennis! You must have said you were taking
the shield for him as a dinner dish ... so where
is it?"

Cousin Dolly opened her eyes. "Why, there
of course!"

She pointed to the cake. Sam and Prune
looked, and Cousin Dolly was right. The cake
was sitting on a small round shield ... a small
round shield decorated with spots, stripes
and zigzags.

"YES!" Sam punched the air. "That's it!"

"DARLING!" Cousin Dolly hugged him, and then hugged Prune. "What joy! How truly and utterly fabulous! Now, just let me find another dish, and you shall have your shield … and we'll have tea and cake to celebrate!"

THINKING FISH

Riding home, the precious shield safely tucked in his saddle bag, Sam noticed Prune was unusually silent. "What's the matter?" he asked.

Prune shrugged. "Nothing."

"Yes, there is," Sam said. "You're always telling me I look like a fish when I'm thinking about something, and now you're doing it too."

Prune heaved a long heavy sigh. "You had a lot of clever ideas today," she said. "You actually had more clever ideas than me. Maybe I'm not a very good True Companion after all."

This was so unlike Prune that Sam pulled Dora to a halt, and stared at his cousin. "But you had LOADS and LOADS of good ideas! It was you that found a way to get here, and it was you that got us past the bats, and it was you that had the idea about the circles – I mean circlets – and it was you ..."

He stopped. Prune was no longer looking like a fish. In fact, far from looking fishlike, she was looking excessively pleased with herself.

"Oh yes," she said. "I did, didn't I? Humph! I'd forgotten."

"I hadn't," Sam said, then paused, and blushed. "I'd say you were the BEST True Companion a knight-in-training could ever have!"

"I am, aren't I?" Prune agreed. "Actually, I always knew I was."

"And tomorrow we'll find out what the fifth task is," Sam said. "Let's hope we don't meet another Dennis!"

"AWK!" said the doodlebird from up above their heads, and Sam and Prune rode on happily together.

Dear Diary,

I was a bit worried that Aunt Egg would be waiting for us when we got home, but she wasn't. She was in the kitchen, wearing an enormous apron, and there was a terrible smell of burning. Aunt Egg was smiling, though. She said she'd made a chicken and Brussels sprout pie, and weren't we lucky? It was a good thing we'd had cake at Cousin Dolly's, because the pie was ABSOLUTELY DISGUSTING. Prune wouldn't eat it at all. I didn't mind, though, because I was so happy! We've done four tasks already!

A True Companion, a snow—white steed, a sword and a shield – maybe I really will get to be a Very Noble Knight after all!

Join Sam and Prune
on their fifth quest!

KNIGHT IN TRAINING

COMBAT AT THE CASTLE

Read on for a sneak peek ...

Hodder
Children's
Books

Dear Diary,

This is probably the very worst day of my life. All I want is to be a Very Noble Knight, and I thought it was REALLY going to happen because I only have two more tasks to do – but it's snowing! And Aunt Egg says Prune and I can't go outside, so I'm stuck here in Mothscale Castle until the sun comes out again. It's boring boring BORING – and I wish Mother and Father had never sent me to stay here. It's freezing cold because Aunt Egg's too mean to light the fires until teatime,

and there's nothing to do. Even the wolves in the forest didn't howl last night – I expect they're all curled up in a nice cosy den. Wish I was in a nice cosy den.

It's SO annoying, because I've done four of the tasks I need to do to be made a knight. I've got my True Companion (my cousin Prune), my snow-white steed (Dora), my sword, and my shield. The magic scroll is hidden under the hay in Aunt Egg's stables (she doesn't know) all ready to tell me and Prune what our next task is – and we can't leave the castle!

Sam pushed his pen away, and stared out of
his bedroom window. Outside, the snowflakes

whirled and twirled as
if they were never
going to stop, and
he sighed a huge
sigh.

"Dandy," he said,
"what do you think'll happen if we can't do the
fifth task today? Will it stop me getting to be a
Very Noble Knight?"

The doodlebird put his head on one side.
"AWK," he said, "AWK."

"Really?" Sam brightened. "We should read
the scroll anyway?"

The doodlebird nodded. "AWK."

"Even though we can't go outside?"

The doodlebird nodded more emphatically.
"AWK!"

Sam jumped up. "I'll go
and find Prune." He hurtled
out of his room and leapt
down the tower stairs.

The doodlebird flew after him, and the
two of them arrived at the bottom in such a
rush that Uncle Archibald, who was coming
out of his study with a pile of books, had to
skip sideways to avoid being flattened. The
books went flying, and Sam skidded to a halt.
"Ooops! Sorry, Uncle Archie." As he began to
pick up the scattered books a title caught his
eye, and he stopped to look at it. "Hey! This is
all about knights! And armour!"

Uncle Archie went pale. "Sssssh!"

Sam didn't hear him. He had opened the book. "I say, Uncle Archie! This is REALLY interesting! It's got all the names for the different bits of armour …"

His uncle was jigging from foot to foot in extreme agitation. "Yes, yes … now, do be a good chap, and stop reading.

Can't have your aunt upset, what what what? Hates it all, don't you know … no time for the past. Wants all my books gone. Burnt." He turned a guilty shade of puce. "Told her I'd done it … but couldn't quite do it at the time."

"So where were you going with them?" Sam asked.

Uncle Archie shook his head, and sighed a gusty sigh. "Kitchen stove. Has to be done. All clear today. Cook's having her rest, and your aunt's feeding the beasts. Prunella's helping her."

Sam was horrified. "But you mustn't burn them! Isn't there somewhere you could hide them? A cellar, or something?"

A thoughtful expression came over Uncle Archibald's face. "The cellar, eh? … Had almost forgotten about the cellar. Not been there for years! Not allowed down the stairs,

of course. Especially on Tuesdays." The old
man shook his head. "Your Aunt Eglantine
– wonderful woman, of course – made me
promise. But there's a cupboard near the top
… should be big enough." He gave Sam a slap
on the back that sent him reeling. "Good lad!
Good lad! Not a word to
your aunt,
mind. Word
of honour?"

GOBLINS

Beware - there are goblins living among us!

Within these pages lies a glimpse into their secret world. But read **quickly**, and speak softly, in case the goblins spot **you**...

A riotous, laugh-out-loud funny series for younger readers from the bestselling author of **HUGLESS DOUGLAS**, David Melling.